ISBN 0 340 17211 8

Copyright © 1973 Gunilla Wolde and Almqvist & Wiksell Förlag AB
English text copyright © 1975 Alison Winn

First published in Great Britain 1975
This impression 1989

Published by Hodder and Stoughton Children's Books,
a division of Hodder and Stoughton Ltd,
Mill Road, Dunton Green, Sevenoaks, Kent TN13 2YJ

Printed in Great Britain by Purnell and Sons (Book Production) Ltd,
Member of BPCC plc, Paulton, Bristol

Co-edition arranged with the help of Angus Hudson, London

Gunilla Wolde

THOMAS
and his cat

English text
Alison Winn

ODDER AND STOUGHTON
NDON SYDNEY AUCKLAND
RONTO

Thomas's Grandma has a cat.

She is a very friendly cat. "Meiou" she says
and rubs herself against Thomas's leg
to show how much she likes him.

Thomas loves stroking pussy's soft silky fur.

Pussy loves being stroked,
she says so by making a loud purring noise.
Thomas thinks it sounds as if
she has a small motor inside her tummy.

Thomas wants to hold pussy.

But pussy doesn't want to be held.
She mews and spits and struggles to get down.
Her tail swishes and she shows her claws.

One of her claws scratches Thomas's arm.
It hurts a bit.

But he soon forgets all about it.
Now Thomas is wondering where pussy has gone.
He wishes she would play with him.

But – pussy doesn't want to play
– she is sitting sulking under Grandma's chair.

Thomas creeps under the chair after her
but pussy gets away.

And hides under Grandma's cupboard instead.

This makes Thomas very cross
– he bangs loudly on the cupboard
but pussy won't come out.

Thomas goes to tell Grandma.
She shows him how to make a special cat toy,
first she folds up a scrap of paper.
And ties a piece of wool round it.

Thomas helps Grandma to make the special cat toy.
When pussy sees the toy she wants to play at once.

Now Thomas snatches the toy away.

But pussy stands up on her back legs
and pats it with her paws.

Suddenly pussy smells *FISH*.
She stops playing to eat her dinner.

Next she laps up a large dish of milk
with her little red tongue.

Washes her face and whiskers.

Stretches out like a piece of elastic.

And curls up on her rug.
With Thomas curled up beside her.

How warm and soft her furry coat feels.
When Thomas strokes her,
the loud purring noise starts again
– louder than ever.

Just look!
Thomas and pussy have both gone to sleep.
Ss'hh – better keep very quiet
so that we don't wake them up.

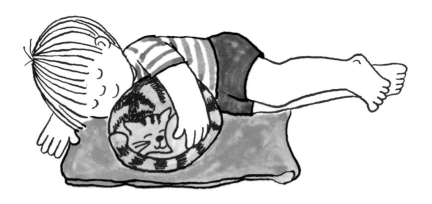